For Marion, fellow author and friend
~ C. F.

For my nephew, Jamie Wernert
~ T. M.

Copyright © 2005 by Good Books, Intercourse, PA 17534
International Standard Book Number: 1-56148-475-X

Library of Congress Catalog Card Number: 2004019532

Text copyright © Claire Freedman 2004
Illustrations copyright © Tina Macnaughton 2004

Original edition published in English by Little Tiger Press,
an imprint of Magi Publications, London, England, 2005.

Printed in China by Leo Paper Products Ltd

Library of Congress Cataloging-in-Publication Data

Freedman, Claire.
Snuggle up, sleepy ones / Claire Freedman; [illustrated by] Tina Macnaughton.
p. cm.
Summary: As night falls in the jungle, all sorts of animals settle down to sleep.
ISBN 1-56148-475-X (hard)
[1. Bedtime--Fiction. 2. Jungle animals--Fiction. 3. Stories in rhyme.]
I. Macnaughton, Tina, ill. II. Title.

PZ8.3.F88Sn 2005
[E]--dc22
2004019532

Snuggle Up, Sleepy Ones

Claire Freedman   Tina Macnaughton

Good Books

Intercourse, PA 17534
800/762-7171
www.goodbks.com

The sun paints the sky
a warm, glowing red.
It's time to stop playing,
it's time for bed.

In the soft swampy mud,
baby hippo, so snug,
Cuddles up close
for a big hippo hug.

Through wild, waving grasses
shy antelope roam.

It's been a long day,
they're ready for home.

Bold leopard cubs rest
from practicing roars.
They snuggle together,
all tired, tangled paws.

While up in the treetops
birds twitter and cheep,

Until quieter and quieter,
they fall fast asleep.

Below in their nests
baby porcupines all
Curl up, snug and tight,
in one spiky ball.

With tired, drooping necks
giraffes flop to the ground.
Sheltered and watched over,
safe and sound.

And mischievous monkeys
shout down from the trees,
"It's not really dark yet.
Five more minutes, please!"

Zebras lie panting,
tired out from their play.
They sink into sleep
as the sun slips away.

Moths go by fluttering,
bats flitter by.
Elephants rumble
their deep lullaby.

Shadows grow deeper,
the lion cubs doze.
Drowsy heads nod,
little eyes start to close.

Stars twinkle brightly,
the moon softly gleams.
Snuggle up, sleepy ones.
Hush now, sweet dreams!